Poppy Love

Poppy Love titles

Poppy Love Steps Out

Poppy Love Faces the Music

Poppy Love Rock 'n' Roll

Poppy Love Star Turn

Poppy Love In the Spotlight

Poppy Love Tango Queen

Poppy Love Goes for Gold

Poppy Love All That Jazz!

Poppy Love Dancing on Air

Poppy Love

Takes the Floor!

NATASHA MAY

illustrated by

SHELAGH MCNICHOLAS

WALKER BOOKS

*With thanks to Neil Kelly and the students of
Rubies Dance Centre
N.M.*

*With thanks to Carolyn, Julia, Kirsty and Ann at
Bell's Dance Centre
S.M.*

First published 2011 by Walker Books Ltd
87 Vauxhall Walk, London SE11 5HJ

2 4 6 8 10 9 7 5 3 1

Text © 2011 Veronica Bennett
Illustrations © 2011 Shelagh McNicholas

The author and illustrator have asserted their moral rights
in accordance with the Copyright, Designs and Patents Act 1988

This book has been typeset in ITC Giovanni

Printed and bound in Great Britain by Clays Ltd, St Ives plc

British Library Cataloguing in Publication Data:
a catalogue record for this book is available from the British Library

ISBN 978-1-4063-2912-4

www.walker.co.uk

Contents

The Last Night

Poppy Love loved ballroom dancing.

For the past two months, she and her partner, Zack Bishop, had been appearing in a professional musical, *Bugsy Malone*. All the parts were played by children. The show had started off in Brighton, the seaside town where Poppy and Zack lived, but was on in London over Christmas. And tonight was the last night.

Poppy and Zack stood on the stage in
a long line of children as the audience
applauded. Forwards and backwards went the
line as the red velvet curtains swung open and
closed, and up and down went the children's
heads as they bowed again and again.

"I'm getting dizzy!" said Poppy to Emma,
her friend from Brighton who was next to her
in the line.

"Here we go again!" said Emma's partner,
Adam, pulling Poppy's hand as the line
surged forwards once more.

The older children who had played the
main parts took their bows one by one.

Poppy watched in admiration as her new friend Amelia and the other leading girls were presented with bunches of flowers, and the boys with single flowers which they stuck in the buttonholes of their wide, 1920s-style lapels.

Then the curtains closed and didn't open again, and soon the applause died away. Poppy could hear muffled footsteps and chatter from the other side of the curtain as the audience began to make their way home.

"I can't believe we're never going to do the show again," said Poppy to Amelia. "We've been together so long, it's going to be strange not seeing you all."

"Oh, I expect you'll see us again!" said Amelia cheerfully.

Poppy wasn't so sure. Amelia went to Burne Hall, a boarding school where the pupils learned dancing, singing and acting. A boy her age called Nick, who came to Miss Johnson's Wednesday evening class, also went to Burne Hall. It was true that Poppy would see *him*, at least until she and her family moved to London next summer. But after that, she might never see any of her friends, old or new, again.

"Anyone at home?" said a voice. It was Zack, looking at Poppy with his head on one side. Poppy shook herself. "Sorry, I was just thinking about—" she began, but was interrupted by a noise like a thunderclap. "What's that?" she asked, looking round.

Two of the men who worked backstage were removing a tall piece of painted wood – called a "flat" – from the side of the stage. The flat had swayed, and fallen loudly against the next one. "Watch it, Pete!" one of the men shouted.

Poppy suddenly noticed that the stage was being cleared and the scenery dismantled. "Everything's disappearing!" she said in surprise.

Nick, who was standing nearby with Amelia, heard Poppy's words. He smiled sympathetically. "It's only a few bits of wood, Poppy," he said.

Poppy knew he was right; another show had to start as soon as possible or the theatre wouldn't make any money. But she couldn't help feeling sad.

For the last three months, *Bugsy Malone* had been the most important thing in her life. She and Zack had rehearsed and performed, hurrying up and down escalators in the Underground, on and off big red buses and along crowded pavements in all kinds of weather. They'd stayed with Dad in his friend's empty flat, sleeping in sleeping-bags on the floor and eating half-burnt sausages and baked beans. Dad wasn't a good cook!

Poppy's make-up and hairbrushes had been laid out in the dressing-room, and her name had appeared in the programme and on the rota at the stage door. She had loved the moment before every performance when the chattering, expectant audience had fallen silent, and the moment when they burst into applause at the end.

And now it was all over.

"So what happens next?" she asked Zack. "Do we just say goodbye and go home?"

Zack frowned. "I suppose so," he said glumly. "Come on, we'd better go and get changed."

Poppy began to follow him off the stage. But suddenly Gary, the director of the show, clapped his hands and said, "Emma's got an announcement to make. Emma?"

Emma stepped forward shyly. "My grandma has invited you all for a party at her house!" she announced.

Another cheer went up. Everyone knew that because Emma lived in Brighton, she was staying with her grandma in London while she performed in *Bugsy*.

"A party *now*?" asked Adam in amazement.

Emma nodded. She began to give out pieces of paper. "Here's the address. I hope everyone can get there."

"Just try and stop us!" said Poppy.

Emma's grandma's house was quite a long way from the theatre.

"It's near an Underground station, though," Poppy's dad told them, "so it's pretty easy to get there."

As she and Zack walked with Dad through the dark streets from the station, Poppy wondered if she'd ever get used to living in London. It seemed to go on and on in all directions. Brighton was tiny in comparison, though she knew it was one of the largest towns in southern England. In Brighton, you could get around without going on a bus or a train. In London, that seemed impossible.

"Dad, are we going to live anywhere near here when we move?" she asked.

"Maybe," he said. "Mum and I have been looking in this area." He pointed to some trees in the distance. "There's a big park with a lake just over there."

Poppy was interested. She would miss living by the sea, but a lake would be nice. "And will I be able to walk to school, like I do now?" she asked.

"I hope so," said Dad.

They stopped at the corner of the street to cross the road. "Look, Mr Love!" said Zack unexpectedly. "This house is for sale!"

The house on the corner had a FOR SALE sign outside it. "So it is!" said Dad, pleased. "And it's the right sort of house, too." He took his phone from his pocket and copied the estate agent's number from the sign. "Thanks, Zack, I'll get the details tomorrow. What do you think, Poppy?"

Poppy looked at the house. It had a shiny green front door with a brass knocker, large front windows and an arched window in the roof. "I like it!" she said.

Zack took a few steps round the corner. "The garden goes back quite a long way," he reported. "Lots of room for Lucky!"

Poppy's puppy, Lucky, lived with her Auntie Jill and Uncle Simon because there was nowhere for him to play outdoors at the Loves' flat in Brighton. Poppy was looking forward to living in a house with a garden so she could have Lucky with her all the time. "Dad, let's buy this house!" she exclaimed.

Dad laughed. "We'll just have to see what happens," he said. He looked at the piece of paper in his hand. "Now, I think Emma's grandma's house is just up here."

As they started walking again, Poppy glanced at Zack. He looked thoughtful. She knew that he was probably thinking that when the Love family moved to London – perhaps to the very house he'd just pointed out – he and Poppy wouldn't see each other much, and might never dance together again.

In fact, now that Zack was so busy at school, he might give up dancing anyway.

"It's a long time till the summer, Zack," she said, and he smiled.

They had reached the house. When Emma's grandma opened the door, Poppy saw that they were almost the last to arrive. The party was so noisy that Emma's grandma, who was a small, elegant lady, almost had to shout. "Hello, I'm Julia Simmonds!"

"I'm Martin Love!" said Dad loudly. "Thank you very much for holding this party!"

Emma appeared while they were taking off their coats. "Hi, Poppy! Hi, Zack!" she said with a welcoming smile. "Come and have some pizza, and ice cream! And we're going to have dancing in a minute!"

The party had divided into two parties,

with the grown-ups chatting in the front room and the children in the room at the back which overlooked the garden. When they went in, Poppy surprised herself by saying, "This is a friendly house!"

"A friendly house?" repeated Zack. "What does that mean?"

Poppy tried to think of a way to explain. "Um ... it's saying 'hello' to us."

"You're bonkers," said Zack, picking up a piece of pizza.

"No, I think I know what Poppy means," said Emma. "Some houses say 'come in' and some houses say 'go away'. And my grandma's house is definitely a 'come in' house, isn't it, Poppy?"

Zack chewed his bite of pizza. "You're both bonkers," he said.

"*There* you are!" cried a familiar voice. It was Amelia, holding Nick's hand. Even in her ordinary clothes, Poppy thought Amelia looked lovely. She was graceful when she moved and lively when she talked, but never behaved in a way Poppy's mum called "pleased with yourself". Though she was two years older than Poppy, she treated her new friend exactly the same as the girls of her own age. "Come on, we need you!" she said to Poppy, Zack and Emma.

"What do you need us for?" asked Zack, beginning on another slice of pizza.

"Nick says no one can do the samba like you," said Amelia, "and we all want to learn."

"Oh, good!" said Poppy. "It seems ages since we did the samba, doesn't it, Zack?"

Emma laughed. "You'd better put that pizza

down, Zack," she said, "and get dancing!"

The chairs were placed against the wall, and the rug rolled up. Poppy and Zack went to the centre of the floor. When Nick started the CD player, the Latin American beat of the samba filled the room. Nick took Emma's hand and they joined Poppy and Zack. "Just listen to the music," he said to the other children, "and copy what we do."

Amelia was dancing with Adam. Neither of them had done Latin American dancing before, but they soon picked up the samba steps. "Hey, Poppy!" Adam called out. "You lot are *good*!"

"Thanks, Adam!" said Poppy. "The samba's fun, isn't it?"

The samba came originally from Brazil, in South America. It was a happy, bouncing dance, famous for being performed at the grand Easter carnival there. Poppy had seen a film of girls dancing the samba dressed in glittering dresses with huge headdresses of feathers. Tonight, although everyone was wearing jeans and sweatshirts, doing the samba still made Poppy think of warm nights in Brazil. It was the perfect party dance!

Poppy and Zack finished doing a back-to-back move and turned to face each other again. "You know, Zack," said Poppy, "I definitely want to be a dancer when I grow up. I never want to do anything else in my whole life!"

Amelia and Adam were passing just as Poppy said this. To Adam's surprise, Amelia stopped dancing, and he almost fell over her.

"Why don't you audition for Burne Hall, then, Poppy?" asked Amelia.

Poppy and Zack stopped dancing too. "What?" said Poppy in astonishment.

"I mean, if you want to be a professional dancer, you'll have a better chance if you train full time," said Amelia. "You're definitely good enough to get in."

Poppy's heart had begun to beat very fast. She had never thought of going to a full-time dance school before, but she was going to be changing school anyway in September, so ...

why not? How fantastic it would be to go to school with Amelia and Nick, and learn not only different kinds of dance, but acting, singing and music too!

She turned to Zack. "What do you think?" she asked.

Zack was thoughtful for a moment, then his face broke into a wide smile. "Yay! Go for it, Pop!" he said.

They began to dance again, but Poppy couldn't keep her mind on her feet. All she could think about was what Amelia had said. Could the end of *Bugsy Malone*, sad though it was, be the beginning of something even more exciting?

Ready for a Challenge

"Look who's here!" said their teacher, Miss Johnson, when Poppy, Zack and Emma appeared for Saturday class at the Blue Horizon Dance Studio.

Their friends gathered round.

"We haven't seen you for *ages*," said Cora, giving Poppy a hug.

"I thought you'd forgotten us!" declared Sam.

"He's only teasing," said Sam's partner, Sophie. "We want to hear all about what you've been doing. It must have been so great, dancing in a London show!"

"It was amazing," said Poppy. "The theatre was huge, but you couldn't see the audience because the lights were shining in your eyes."

"You could hear them, though!" said Zack. "When they applauded it sounded like a stampede of dinosaurs!"

"And dancing to a live orchestra was great!" added Emma.

"Which bit did you like best?" Cora asked them.

Poppy thought. "Getting ready to go on, I think," she told her friend. "Wishing everyone luck, and just ... being there!"

"I liked the dresses!" added Emma.

"I liked getting paid," declared Zack. "And eating sausages and beans in the middle of the night."

Miss Johnson laughed. "It sounds like quite an experience," she said. "I expect you were sad when it ended, weren't you?"

Zack and Emma nodded. "Definitely," said Emma.

But Poppy didn't reply. She wasn't sure what to say. In a way, she *was* sad that the show had to end. But in another way, she was glad to be back. And there was a lot to look forward to before the Love family moved away from Brighton – Auntie Jill's baby would be born, and there would be events and parties for Poppy and her friends in the top year at Linden Tree Junior School. The others would go on to secondary school in Brighton next September. But where would Poppy go to school?

She hadn't mentioned Burne Hall to Mum and Dad yet, though she thought about it all the time. Amelia had told her that the auditions took place in a couple of months. But it was so nice being at home! She couldn't decide whether to ask her parents if she could do the audition, or forget all about it.

"Now, let me tell you what's happening next Saturday," Miss Johnson said to Poppy, Zack and Emma.

"We're going to be dancing in a show for the mayor!" exclaimed Sophie, before Miss Johnson could go on. "And lots of other people, of course."

"At the Dome!" added Sam proudly.

Brighton Dome was a large concert hall, and the mayor was an important person. "Wow!" exclaimed Zack. "What's going on?"

"It's a special performance," explained Miss Johnson, "in aid of a children's charity. Children from all over Brighton are going to be dancing, singing, playing music, all sorts of things. Would you three like to dance in the show too?" she asked.

Poppy and Emma looked at each other and nodded eagerly, and Zack said, "We'd love it!"

"You can do a Charleston, like you did in *Bugsy*," said Miss Johnson. "I've got some Charleston costumes somewhere."

"Great!" exclaimed Emma. "I'll get to wear a pretty dress again!"

* * *

The dresses for the Charleston routine were perfect. Poppy's was pink and Emma's blue, and they each had a matching headband with a feather in it. As they waited in the wings at the Dome on Saturday, they wiggled their hips to make the hem of their short skirts flip.

"These costumes are so cool!" said Emma.

Poppy looked across the stage to where Zack was waiting. "Zack looks cool too, doesn't he?"

He had on black trousers, a black shirt, a white tie and a trilby hat. "Every bit the gangster!" Miss Johnson had said.

Their teacher had made up a routine in which Emma and Poppy had to pretend to fight over who was going to dance with Zack.

He did some clowning around with the hat, then they all danced together for the rest of the routine.

"He really likes that hat!" giggled Emma. "Do you think he'll start wearing it all the time?"

When the music began, Poppy and Emma ran into the centre of the stage and swung into the Charleston, a 1920s dance where they had to keep their feet placed but their knees loose, so that the dance looked relaxed and carefree. The music was so bouncy, Poppy was sure it would make everyone in the audience tonight want to get up and dance too! Even the mayor!

At the end of the Charleston routine, the audience clapped, whistled and cheered. And at the end of the show, when the mayor made a speech about how talented Brighton children were, he said, "And special thanks goes to three young professionals, fresh from their recent appearance in London – Emma Feltham, Poppy Love and Zack Bishop!"

Poppy felt very shy while everyone clapped again, but she loved hearing that word, "professional". It meant that for the few weeks that *Bugsy Malone* was on, she'd been a real dancer. Wouldn't it be fantastic to follow in Auntie Jill's footsteps and be a professional dancer when she grew up?

Maybe going to Burne Hall *was* a good idea.

Mum came to see the show. Afterwards, as they were walking back to the car, Poppy tugged her mother's hand. "Can I talk to you about something?" she asked.

"Of course you can," replied Mum, stopping.

"I wonder if I'm good enough to get into Burne Hall?" asked Poppy. The words came out in a rush, with a kind of hiccup in the middle because she was too nervous to breathe.

Mum looked at Poppy in surprise. "Why do you say that?" she said. "Are you thinking of auditioning? You know it's a boarding school, don't you?"

"Yes," said Poppy, beginning to breathe again. "But I'd still like to go. I want to be a professional dancer, like Auntie Jill."

"You can do that without training full time, you know," said Mum thoughtfully.

"But I want to learn all kinds of dancing, and singing, like Amelia and Nick," said Poppy, "and perform on stage lots more."

Mum smiled. "In that case," she said, "I think we should speak to Dad, and Auntie Jill. And we'd better ask Miss Johnson what she thinks, too."

Poppy thought this was a brilliant idea. "Oh, yes!" she agreed. "Thank you!"

"But if we decide to say no," added Mum as they hurried towards the car park, "then no means no."

Poppy understood this. But she crossed the fingers of the hand that wasn't holding her mum's hand. She so hoped they would say yes!

* * *

A few weeks later,
Miss Johnson, Auntie
Jill, Mum, Dad, Tom
and Poppy gathered
in the living room for a

discussion about the audition for Burne Hall.
Poppy felt a little strange, knowing that all
these people were here because of *her*.

"Poppy has a good chance of getting in,"
said Miss Johnson. "She's very talented."

Poppy wriggled with embarrassment as
everyone looked at her. It was odd, being
talked about as if she wasn't there.

"When's the audition?" asked Tom.

Miss Johnson looked at the details Burne
Hall had sent. "Saturday the thirtieth of
April," she said. "That gives us about a
month to prepare."

A month! It didn't sound very long. "What will I have to do?" asked Poppy.

"First of all, a ballet class," replied her teacher. "Then, in the afternoon, each child performs a solo in costume, in the dance style they like best."

"In front of the whole class?" asked Poppy, dismayed.

"Oh, no!" replied Miss Johnson hurriedly. "Only for the teachers. They want to see you perform a piece of choreography, and act a character."

Poppy was relieved. "I can do that!" she said.

"Some of the girls will do a ballet solo," said Miss Johnson, "and some will do tap, and some jazz or modern. But I wonder how many of them will do..."

She stopped, smiling at Poppy expectantly.

"*Ballroom!*" said Poppy. She thought fast. "A paso doble?" she suggested. In the paso doble, a Latin American dance, the boy acted the part of a matador. "I won't have a matador, but I can imagine him. I know, I can be his *cape!*" went on Poppy.

"That would certainly show performance and character," agreed Miss Johnson. "And imagination, too."

"Let's start tomorrow!" cried Poppy.

"Wait a moment, Poppy," said Mum. "We haven't even agreed to the audition yet. Do you know what being at a boarding school means?"

"Yes," said Poppy. "I would sleep at Burne Hall every night and come home in the holidays."

"And how would you like that?" asked Dad.

Poppy knew she would find it very strange to live away from home. She would miss Mum and Dad and Tom, and Auntie Jill and Uncle Simon, very much. "I don't know," she told her dad. "But it would mean I can dance, and learn singing, and acting!"

"You have to do ordinary school subjects as well, Poppy," said Auntie Jill. "Maths and History and Science, and so on. It's very hard work."

Poppy hadn't thought of this. "But if the other children can do it, then so can I," she said.

Mum looked at Auntie Jill. "What do you think, Jill?" she asked.

38

"I think," said Auntie Jill, smiling at Poppy, "that Poppy loves dancing so much, she'd be very happy at Burne Hall."

Mum nodded and looked at Dad. "What do you think?" she asked.

Dad began to walk about the room, as he always did when he was thinking. Tom chewed his lip. Poppy held her breath.

"If you don't like it," said Dad to Poppy, "you can always come home and go to an ordinary school. OK?"

"OK," agreed Poppy.

Dad stopped walking about. "Tom?" he said, looking at Poppy's brother expectantly.

"If you don't do the audition, Poppy." said Tom, "you'll never know if you were good enough, for ever and ever. That would be *awful*."

They all looked at Mum, who had been listening carefully. She put her arm around Poppy's shoulders. "How about this?" she said. "Why don't we enter you for the audition, and then you and Miss Johnson have got a month to prepare. During that month, you can always change your mind."

Poppy was very relieved her mum hadn't said no. "Thanks, Mum!" she said.

"I'd miss you very much, Poppy," said Mum softly.

"I'd miss you too," said Poppy.

Just then, they heard the front door slam. "Hello!" called Uncle Simon.

The living-room door was nudged open by a small, wet nose, and the front half of Lucky appeared around it. He looked at them with his head on one side, as if to say, "What are you all doing here without me?"

Poppy picked him up. "Uncle Simon, you didn't tell me you were bringing Lucky!" she said.

Then she remembered something that she should have thought of before, but somehow, in all the excitement, she'd forgotten. "Oh!" she exclaimed. "If I go to boarding school, I'll be apart from Lucky again, just when we're moving to a house with a garden so that I can be *with* him!"

For a moment, she felt like crying. Why couldn't Burne Hall be a day school?

"Does that mean you don't want to audition after all?" asked Dad.

Poppy didn't cry. She put Lucky down and looked at Dad. "No," she said firmly. "Lucky's lovely, but I won't change my mind."

"That's my Poppy!" said Dad proudly. "Always ready for a challenge!"

The Biggest Thing
in the World

On the day of the audition, Poppy woke up
with butterflies in her stomach. When Mum
came in to do her hair, she was sitting on the
edge of her bed, saying her eight times table
to herself, trying to think about anything
except the audition.

"Six eights are forty-eight," she chanted.
"Seven eights are..." She couldn't think.
"What are seven eights?" she asked Mum.

"Just add eight to forty-eight," said Mum. "And come and sit on the stool."

Poppy sat in front of her mirror and Mum began to brush her hair into a pony-tail. Poppy tried to add eight to forty-eight, but her brain didn't want to think about arithmetic. It was too busy imagining the audition class.

"What if I make a mistake?" she asked.

"Everyone makes mistakes," said Mum.

This didn't make Poppy feel much better. "What if I fall over?" she asked.

"You'll get up again, like you always do," said Mum. "Now, keep still while I put this bun net on. And by the way, there's a surprise waiting for you in the kitchen."

This *did* make Poppy feel better. When
she was dressed, she ran into the kitchen.
On the table were three envelopes, each one
addressed to *Miss P. Love*. Inside the first
one was a good luck card from Granny and
Grandad, decorated with red poppies, and
in the second envelope was one from Auntie
Jill, Uncle Simon and Lucky.
The puppy had put one of
his muddy paws on the
card, which made Poppy laugh.

She had left the biggest envelope until
last. When she opened it, she gasped. It
was a home-made card, with *Good Luck,
Poppy!* written across the front in glittery
letters. Inside was written "Lots and lots of
lucky love!" Zack had signed it, and he had
also drawn a cartoon of Poppy dancing.

Underneath his name were those of all her friends at the Blue Horizon – Sophie, Sam, Cora, Luke, Little Tom, Emma, Nick, Rosie and Debbie, with messages and drawings all around.

Poppy held the card to her chest and hugged it. Some of the glitter came off on her ballet cardigan but she didn't care. "Look at my beautiful cards!" she said as her mum came into the room. "Let's take them with us!"

Poppy didn't know if it was the cards that did it, but she found that her butterflies had vanished by the time she entered the studio at

Burne Hall. She just felt happy to be there, lining up with the other girls along the barre, with the number 16 pinned to the front and back of her leotard.

The tall, slim teacher who was taking the audition class told them to call her Miss Taylor. "Although, as I don't know your names," she added, "I'm afraid I'll have to call you by your numbers."

Two other teachers were sitting at the side of the room. Poppy recognized Miss Ford, who

 had taught her last year when she had attended summer school at Burne Hall. She knew she mustn't let the other dancers know, as it would be unfair. So she didn't smile at Miss Ford, but gazed calmly at the back of the head of the girl in front of her, ready to begin.

Miss Johnson had explained to Poppy that as Burne Hall wasn't a ballet school, they weren't expecting anyone to perform immaculate ballet steps. But ballet was the basis of all dancing because it taught dancers how to control their bodies. By watching a ballet class, the teachers could tell which girls had strong middles, held their heads and limbs well, kept in time with the music, and copied the teacher's steps correctly. All the things that made a beautiful dancer!

The girls did exercises at the barre, facing first one way, then the other. They did the same exercises in the centre of the floor, and some step sequences. Poppy could see that Miss Taylor and the other teachers were watching everyone very carefully.

After the class they had lunch, and then

the girls and their parents were shown round the dormitories, where the students slept. To Poppy's delight, lots of the students had left teddy bears, dance shoes or cards on their beds with good luck messages for the girls who were auditioning.

"Isn't that lovely of them?" said Mum. "Where are they all today, I wonder?"

The older girl who was showing them the dormitory heard Mum's question. "They've gone home for the weekend," she explained. "A lot of us only stay here during the week."

Mum squeezed Poppy's arm. "There, Poppy!" she said happily. "If you did that, you'd be able to see Lucky every weekend. And us, of course."

"Now I want to come here even more!" said Poppy.

In the afternoon, the girls did their solos. Mum helped Poppy put on her long swirly dress with the sleeves made to look like a cape. Real matadors' capes were red or pink, but the dress was in different shades of purple. The colour really suited Poppy, with her dark hair, and she knew the layers in the skirt would look good when she started to move.

She looked at her reflection. Her hair was in a bun, and Mum had put lilac flowers in it. Poppy's face was made up to look Spanish, with dark eyeliner and red lips. "I wish Miss Johnson was here," she said. "She'd say, 'Ready to enter the bullring?'"

"She's thinking about you, I'm sure," said Mum. "And so are Zack and your friends."

Poppy looked again at her cards, especially the one from Zack. She would miss him.

But she knew in her heart that wherever she went, there would be people who wanted to be friends, like those kind Burne Hall students who had left messages on their beds.

"Time to go," said Mum.

Poppy went into the studio and took up her paso doble position in front of the teachers. They smiled, but she didn't smile back. When you're acting a character, Miss Johnson always said, it starts the moment you take up the dance position, and it doesn't end until after the music has stopped. A matador's cape had serious business, and never, *never* smiled.

The music began. Poppy dipped her head, then raised it. Her skirt whirled around her legs as she took her first steps.

The paso doble needed her to make firm strides, holding her head up and arching her back. She showed off the cape effect of her dress, swirling the material around as the imaginary bull charged again and again, putting her arms out sideways so that the half circle of the cape could be seen. And all the time, her feet in their silver dancing shoes stamped and clicked their way neatly through the steps of the paso doble.

At the end, the "cape" lay on the floor where the matador had left it. Poppy stayed there for a few more moments, then she got up and curtseyed to the three watching teachers. To her surprise, they applauded.

"Well done, Poppy," said Miss Ford, smiling widely. "You're free to go now. You'll receive a letter in a few days."

Poppy was dismayed. A few days! She curtseyed again and left the studio.

Mum was waiting expectantly in the dressing-room. "How did it go?" she asked.

"I think it went OK," replied Poppy. Suddenly, she felt mixed up inside. Her happy mood had gone, and in its place was a flat feeling, like a let-down balloon.

Mum looked concerned. "Are you all right, love?" she asked.

"I just want to go home," Poppy said.

"You're not changing your mind about coming here, are you?" asked Mum, beginning to unzip Poppy's dress.

Poppy turned so fast that the zip almost tore the material. "No!" she said. "Oh, Mum, getting into Burne Hall is ... it's the biggest thing in the world!"

* * *

"Poppy!" said Dad impatiently. "Calm down! You're 'popping' about all over the place like a firework!"

Poppy knew she was being annoying, but she couldn't sit still. She was unable to settle to read, or watch TV, or help Mum cook lunch, or any of the things she usually did on a Sunday. Uncle Simon had brought Lucky over, but they hadn't stayed long because Auntie Jill wasn't feeling very well, so Poppy didn't even have her puppy to play with.

"Sorry, Dad," she said.

He caught hold of her as she passed his chair. "Look, I know it's hard, waiting for this letter," he said. "But think about it, sweetheart. It's Sunday today, so the teachers won't be there. Tomorrow they'll start deciding who passed the audition and who didn't, and then the letters have got to be written and posted. It might take a week. So try not to think about it too much."

"How can I make myself not think about it?" asked Poppy, sitting on the arm of Dad's chair.

"Here," he said. "Read this and tell me what you think."

He handed her a piece of paper. On it was a photograph of a house, with smaller pictures and some information about the house underneath. Poppy suddenly realized what she was looking at. "This is the house Zack found! Are we going to live there?" she asked eagerly.

"I hope so," said Dad. "Mum and I have been to see it a couple of times, and we've offered to buy it. We thought we'd take you and Tom to see it after school later this week."

Poppy studied the pictures. "It's a friendly house," she said. "Just like Emma's grandma's house."

"Glad to hear it," said Dad. He pointed to one of the pictures. "Look, this could be your room. Why don't you think about how you want it decorated?"

Poppy was interested. Even if she went to Burne Hall, she would be at home every weekend, and it would be nice to have a newly decorated bedroom. "So when will we know, definitely, if we're going to live here?" she asked.

"Soon, unless something goes wrong," said Dad. "Cross your fingers."

Poppy crossed her fingers. "Have I got to keep them crossed until we move in?" she asked.

"Of course," teased Dad. "Even when you're asleep."

Poppy sighed. "I don't think I'm going to be able to sleep," she said. "Not until I get that letter!"

The family who lived in the new house were away, so a smartly dressed man from the estate agent's met the Loves outside and let them in.

The room that might be
Poppy's had wallpaper
with bunnies and
kittens on it, but Poppy
could see the garden
from the window.
"I like it!" she said.
"Er ... with different wallpaper, I mean."
Mum laughed. "The children who live here
are a lot younger than you and

Tom," she said.
Tom opened
the door to
"his" room. It
had a high bed
with a ladder
and a picture of
Spider-Man on the

duvet cover. "You can tell," he said.

"This house *is* friendly," declared Poppy, "just like I said." Eagerly, she followed Tom and Dad up the stairs to the attic, where the Loves planned to have a den. Part of the attic was for storage, but the other part was a large room with an arched window overlooking the street.

"There's so much space!" said Poppy, looking round.

"I know," said Mum, who had just reached the top of the attic stairs. "Isn't it great? When I—"

Poppy never found out what her mother had been going to say next, because Mum's phone rang. When she answered it, her eyes widened. "Oh!" she said in surprise. "Oh, Simon! Yes, we'll be there as soon as we can."

She closed the phone. There were joyful tears in her eyes. "Jill's had the baby!" she told them. "It's a healthy, beautiful boy!"

"We've got a cousin, Poppy!" said Tom.

Poppy was confused. Auntie Jill's baby wasn't supposed to come for another couple of weeks. "But it's two weeks too soon!" she exclaimed as she and Tom followed their parents downstairs.

"Two weeks early or late doesn't make much difference to babies," explained Mum. She smiled at Poppy. "Isn't it exciting?"

It was exciting. Poppy was impatient to see the new baby, but there was a lot of traffic on the road to Brighton, and the journey was very slow. Mum was even more impatient – she was thrilled that she had a nephew!

"Mum, you know I said getting into Burne Hall's the biggest thing in the world?" said Poppy. "Well, I'm beginning to think that Auntie Jill having a baby is even bigger!"

Dad agreed. "It's certainly taken your mind off that letter, hasn't it?" he said.

A New Life

The only time Poppy had ever been in the hospital in Brighton was when she was born. It was a brightly lit building with wide corridors and shiny floors. People were scurrying this way and that, some of them pushing trolleys or wheelchairs. "Where will the baby be?" she asked as they went through the automatic doors.

"Don't worry," said Mum. "We'll find him."

The lady at the reception desk directed them to the right part of the hospital. The corridors were very long, and they all looked the same, but at last they arrived at some doors that said MATERNITY WING, and Mum pushed them open. There was Uncle Simon, waiting for them! He looked hot and his hair hadn't been combed, but his face was covered with a huge grin. "I'm a dad!" he said happily.

Dad shook his hand and Mum hugged him so hard she almost knocked his glasses off. Poppy jumped up and down in excitement. "Where's the baby?" she asked. "And Auntie Jill?"

"She's asleep, so the baby's in the nursery,"
said Uncle Simon, straightening his glasses.
"Come along and see him."

The nursery was a room with a big window
on to the corridor. It was full of cots, each
containing a tiny baby. Some cots had pink
stickers on them and some had blue. On
one of the blue ones was written BABY BOY
FORRESTER.

"That's him!" exclaimed Poppy, pointing.
"Look, Tom, there's our cousin!"

A nurse wheeled Baby Boy Forrester's cot
out, and Poppy peered into it. The sleeping
baby was lying with his face to one side,
breathing gently. His little chest went up
and down with each
breath, and his tiny
nose twitched.

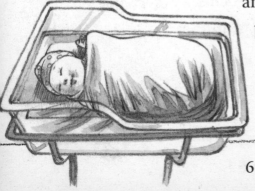

He had one of his hands up by his cheek. Poppy was amazed at his fingers, so small but so perfectly formed. She thought she had never seen anything more beautiful than this little boy. "He's *gorgeous*!" she said.

"Well, I think so," said Uncle Simon proudly.

Mum had tears in her eyes again. "We all do, Simon," she said, looking fondly at her new nephew. "Congratulations."

"What's his name?" asked Tom suddenly.

No one had thought of that. They all looked at Uncle Simon. "We're not sure," he said, "but Jill and I like Archie."

Poppy looked at the baby. "He's an Archie," she said. "He's *definitely* an Archie."

Uncle Simon smiled. "I think maybe he is," he said.

They stayed a little longer, then Dad said, "You'd better get some sleep, Simon." He shook Uncle Simon's hand again. "We'll come back and see Jill tomorrow."

Poppy stroked the baby's little hand softly. "Good night, Archie," she said.

That night, Poppy dreamed peculiar dreams full of bunnies and kittens, and babies' fingers and hospital corridors, and Spider-Man and an arched window, all mixed up. When she woke up in the morning, the first thing she thought of was her new cousin. Mum had promised that they'd all go to see Archie and Auntie Jill after school. Poppy jumped out of bed, and almost slipped on a white envelope that had been on her bed but had fallen to the floor.

She picked it up. It was addressed to Mum

and Dad, but it hadn't been opened. They must want *her* to open it. Her heart raced as she turned the envelope over. In small letters on the back was printed BURNE HALL SCHOOL FOR THE PERFORMING ARTS.

With shaky fingers she tore open the envelope. Inside were several sheets of paper with a letter on top. Poppy had only read the first line when she began to jump up and down, whooping and shrieking so loudly that within a few seconds Mum, Dad and Tom were in her room.

"I got in!" she told them, half crying, half laughing. *"I got in!"*

Dad picked her up and hugged her. "My clever, talented girl!" he said.

Mum kissed Poppy over and over again, and even Tom was pleased. He hopped around Poppy's room with one of his school shoes on and the other off, saying to no one in particular "Hah!" and "Ho!"

When the excitement had died down, Poppy sat on her bed and looked at the letter properly. There was too much information to read it all now, as she had to get ready for school. Her best friend, Mia, would want to hear all about it. But tonight, she decided, she'd read every word. Twice, at least.

While she was getting dressed, Poppy thought about Mia, and wondered if she'd ever see her again after they left Linden Tree Junior School.

Soon, she'd have to say goodbye to Miss Johnson and all her friends at the Blue Horizon too. With her school dress half on and her hairbrush in her hand, she opened her bedroom door and called down the passage to Mum.

"What is it, love?" asked Mum, her head appearing around the kitchen door.

Poppy wasn't quite sure what she wanted to say. "Um..." she began.

Mum came out of the kitchen, drying her hands on a tea towel. "Are you OK?" she asked.

Poppy nodded. "I'm fine," she said. "In fact, I'm really happy. It's just that I'm leaving so many people behind. How can I be sorry to say goodbye to them, and happy that I'm going, both at the same time?"

Mum put the tea towel over her shoulder and took Poppy's hand. "Come on, you need to hurry. I'll help you do your hair. And don't worry," she said as they went into Poppy's room, "I think I know a very happy way to say goodbye."

The private function room at the Gemini Hotel was usually decorated for wedding receptions on Saturdays. But on this particular Saturday, a few weeks later, it was being used for something else. The trouble was, Poppy wasn't sure what.

"We're having a celebration," Mum told her. "Because we've got lots of things to celebrate. The new house, the new baby, Burne Hall, Uncle Simon and Auntie Jill taking over the hotel..."

"A party, you mean?" asked Poppy.

"Wait and see," was all Mum would say.

No one would let Poppy join in the preparations. On the day of the "celebration", Mum told her to stay upstairs until two o'clock, when it began.

"What shall I wear?" she asked Auntie Jill. Uncle Simon was helping in the hotel while Poppy and her auntie looked after Archie. There wasn't much looking after to do just now, as he was fast asleep.

Auntie Jill put her head on one side and studied Poppy for a moment. "Why not put on one of your dancing dresses?" she suggested. "The pink one you had for Blackpool when you won the gold medal, perhaps?"

"But it's not a party dress," said Poppy, puzzled. Then she remembered her mum hadn't actually said they were having a *party*. "So shall I wear my dancing shoes too?" she asked.

"Good idea," said Auntie Jill.

Poppy didn't ask any more questions, but as she went to her room to get the pink dress out of the wardrobe, there were butterflies in her tummy. Just what was Mum planning? Would everyone else be dressed in dancing clothes, or just Poppy? Why wouldn't they tell her what was going on?

She took the dress out of its plastic bag and shook out the folds. It did look pretty. She hoped it still fitted her. Holding it against herself as she looked in the mirror, she danced a few steps, remembering how wonderful it had been when she and Zack had won the Stardance competition at the Nationwide Finals in Blackpool last year.

It had been great dancing with him for medal tests, displays and festivals, too. They'd performed so many times, Poppy could hardly remember all of the occasions. But what she did remember was the way Zack pretended he wasn't nervous when he was, how funny he was sometimes, how he called her "Pop", and how he threw himself into his dancing. He was always determined to do his best for Miss Johnson, and for Poppy.

She swished the skirt of the dress, thinking about other dresses and headdresses, sparkly shoes, make-up, hairspray and fake tan.

It had all been so much fun, getting ready at competitions with the other girls – Sophie, with her round face and fair hair, lively Cora and her corkscrew curls, beautiful Emma, friendly older girls Rosie and Debbie. And the boys – daft Sam, quiet Luke and Uncle Simon's easy-going nephew, Little Tom. How strange it would be, never seeing any of them again! And how Poppy would miss them!

There was a knock on Poppy's door, and it opened a little bit. "Does the dress still fit?" asked Auntie Jill.

"I haven't tried it on yet," admitted Poppy. "But it looks fine. Is Archie still asleep?"

Auntie Jill nodded. "I've got an idea," she said, coming into the room. "Let's put your hair up with the pink decoration that matches the dress. And how about some lipstick?"

By the time Poppy was ready, it was past two o'clock. Auntie Jill picked up Archie. "Let's go," she said, whispering in case the baby awoke.

"Do I look OK?" asked Poppy

"You look *lovely*," Auntie Jill told her. "Ready?"

They left Archie and Uncle Simon behind the reception desk, then Auntie Jill took Poppy's hand and knocked importantly on the closed doors of the function room. To Poppy's surprise, the doors opened slowly from the inside. She felt her auntie gently nudge her, and she took one step into the room. But she didn't take any more because she was too surprised to move. She looked around, gasped, put her hand over her mouth, took it off again and said, "Wow!"

The whole room was covered with poppies. There were chains of paper poppies hanging from the ceiling and draped around the walls. A long table, loaded with party food, was strewn with poppy petals. Poppy could hardly believe it, but Mia, Sophie, Cora, Emma and all the other girls were wearing garlands of paper poppies around their heads. And every boy was proudly wearing a red poppy on his chest – except Zack, who had put his behind his ear to make Poppy laugh.

She did laugh. She cried a bit, too. She was so overwhelmed, she hardly knew *what* to do. "A Poppy party!" she exclaimed, hugging Mum. "What a brilliant idea! Thanks, Mum!"

To Poppy's delight, Amelia and

Nick were there. Amelia, looking beautiful
in her red poppy garland, threw her arms
around Poppy.

"I *knew* you'd pass the audition!"
she cried. "We're so looking
forward to seeing you at Burne
Hall next term!"

"I'll have someone to practise
my ballroom dancing with every day," said
Nick. Then, to Poppy's surprise, he caught
her up in the waltz position. "And talking of
ballroom dancing," he said, "may I have the
pleasure, Miss Love?"

Someone started the waltz music and Nick
led Poppy to the centre of the floor. "So
that's why Auntie Jill wanted me to wear my
dancing dress!" thought Poppy as they began
the swaying, romantic dance.

Other dancers joined them. Then suddenly,
Nick seemed to melt away, and
Zack appeared in front of
Poppy with the biggest smile
she'd ever seen. "Ready, Pop?"
he asked.

Poppy and Zack circled
the floor. As always, it felt
perfect dancing with him,
and Poppy couldn't help smiling. Although
she knew their partnership would soon
have to come to an end, she didn't feel sad.
Dancing with Zack had brought her lots of

exciting experiences, and
so much fun. Now, they
both had new things to do.
How could she feel anything
but happiness?

Suddenly, Poppy heard the sound of a baby crying. Archie had woken up and Uncle Simon had brought him in.

"Zack..." began Poppy, watching Auntie Jill pick up the baby. "I've just thought of something. Archie's not the only one with a new life, is he? My whole family has a new life. We're moving to a new house in a new place, and I've got my own new life at Burne Hall." She stopped waltzing and looked at Zack. "Your life'll be different too, won't it?" she added. "Everything's changing."

Zack looked back at her. His eyes were very bright. "Not quite *everything*," he said. "Poppy Love will always, *always* love to dance!"

Natasha May loves dance of all kinds. When she was a little girl she dreamed of being a dancer, but also wanted to be a writer. "So writing about dancing is the best job in the world," she says. "And my daughter, who is a dancer, keeps me on my toes about the world of dance."

Shelagh McNicholas loves to draw people spinning around and dancing. Her passion began when her daughter, Molly, started baby ballet classes, "and as she perfected her dancing skills we would practise the jive, samba and quickstep all around the house!"